A NOTE TO PARENTS

Disney's First Readers Level 2 books were created for beginning readers who are gaining confidence in their early reading skills.

Compared to Level 1 books, **Level 2** books have slightly smaller type and contain more words to a page. Although sentence structure is still simple, the stories are slightly longer and more complex.

Just as children need training wheels when learning to ride a bicycle, they need the support of a good model when learning to read. Every time your child sees that you enjoy reading, whether alone or with him or her, you provide the encouragement needed to build reading confidence. Here are some helpful hints to use with the **Disney's First Readers Level 2** books:

★ Play or act out each character's words. Change your voice to indicate which character is speaking. As your child becomes comfortable with the printed text, he or she can take a favorite character's part and read those passages.

★ Have your child try reading the story. If your child asks about a word, do not interrupt the flow of reading to make him or her sound it out. Pronounce the word for your child. If, however, he or she begins to sound it out, be gently encouraging—your child is developing phonetic skills!

★ Read aloud. It's still important at this level to read to your child. With your child watching, move a finger smoothly along the text. Do not stop at each word. Change the tone of your voice to indicate punctuation marks, such as questions and exclamations. Your child will begin to notice how words and punctuation marks make sense and can make reading fun.

★ Let your child ask you questions about the story. This will help to develop your child's critical thinking skills. Use the After-Reading Fun activities provided at the end of each book as a fun exercise to further enhance your child's reading skills.

★ Praise all reading efforts warmly and often!

Remember that early-reading experiences that you share with your child can help him or her to become a confident and successful reader later on!

— Patricia Koppman
Past President
International Reading Association

Pencils by Scott Tilley and Denise Shimabukoro

First published by Disney Press, New York, New York.
This edition published by Scholastic Inc.,
90 Old Sherman Turnpike, Danbury, Connecticut 06816
by arrangement with Disney Licensed Publishing.

SCHOLASTIC and associated logos are trademarks of Scholastic Inc.

ISBN 0-7172-8898-6

Printed in the U.S.A.

Abu Monkeys Around

by Anne Schreiber
Illustrated by Darren Hont

Disney's First Readers — Level 2
A Story from Disney's *Aladdin*

★★

SCHOLASTIC INC.

New York   Toronto   London   Auckland   Sydney
Mexico City   New Delhi   Hong Kong   Buenos Aires

From Monday,
when the week began,
to Sunday, at its end,

Abu played tricks on the Genie
and all of the Genie's friends.

On Monday,
everyone was sleeping.

Except Abu.
BANG!

Abu banged the lamp.
It started to shake.
It fell on the floor.
Is the Genie awake?

On Tuesday,
everyone was dressing.

Except Abu.
CLANG!

Abu scared the Genie
by ringing a bell.
The Genie jumped up.
Down Abu fell.

On Wednesday,
everyone was eating.

Except Abu.
CRASH!

Abu spilled the juice.
He dropped the fruit.

The Genie got juice
all over his suit.

On Thursday,
everyone was resting.

Except Abu.
SPLASH!

Abu jumped in the water.
He wanted to swim.
Aladdin got wet.
The Genie fell in.

On Friday,
everyone was shopping.

Except Abu.
WHOOSH!

Abu left a mess
on the ground.
His friends walked by
and slid all around.

On Saturday,
everyone was working.

Except Abu.
SWOOSH!

Abu jumped on a cart
to grab a sweet treat.

He knocked the cart over
Apples rolled down
the street.

What has Abu done?

On Monday he woke the Genie.
On Tuesday he made things crash.
On Wednesday he spilled the juice.
On Thursday he made a splash.
On Friday he left a mess,
and all his friends fell down.
On Saturday he jumped on a cart
and spilled apples on the ground.

On Sunday, when the
week was through,
no one could sleep.
ZZZzzzzzzzzzzzz.

Except Abu.

AFTER-READING FUN

Enhance the reading experience with follow-up questions to help your child develop reading comprehension and increase his/her awareness of words.

Approach this with a sense of play. Make a game of having your child answer the questions. You do not need to ask all the questions at one time. Let these questions be fun discussions rather than a test. If your child doesn't have instant recall, encourage him/her to look back into the book to "research" the answers. You'll be modeling what good readers do and, at the same time, forging a sharing bond with your child.

1. What did Abu do on Monday?

2. On what day of the week was everyone shopping?

3. How would you describe Abu's behavior?

4. Why do you think everyone is happy when Abu falls asleep?

5. What words in this story describe sounds?

6. Find a rhyming word for shake, bell, fruit, around, and treat.

Answers: 1. he woke the genie. 2. Friday. 3. *possible answers:* playful, naughty, frisky; he likes to play tricks. 4. Abu finally stopped playing tricks. 5. bang, clang, crash, splash, whoosh, swoosh. 6. *possible answers:* shake-awake; bell-fell; fruit-suit; around-ground; treat-street.